El Toro Pinto

El Toro Pinto

and
Other Songs in Spanish

Selected and illustrated by Anne Rockwell

ALADDIN PAPERBACKS

Grateful acknowledgment is made to the following publishers and copyright holders for permission to reprint copyrighted music and Spanish lyrics:

Academy Library Guild, Sausalito, California, for "Cielito Lindo," from *Spanish Folksongs of the Southwest,* collected by Mary R. Van Stone; The John Day Company for "Baile de Nadal," "Niña, Nana," "La Panaderita," "Era una Vez," "¡Jeu! ¡Jeu!" and "El Tortillero," from *Folk Songs of the World,* edited by John Haywood, The John Day Company, 1966; Ginn and Company for "A Cantar a una Niña" and "Arroz con Leche," from *The Latin-American Song Book,* copyright 1942 by Ginn and Company, used with permission; Abelardo Gutierrez, Medellin, Colombia, for "El Zancudo" and "Mi Compadre Mono"; George G. Harrap & Co., Ltd., for "El Sol y la Luna," from *Cancionero Musical Español* by Eduardo M. Turner, George G. Harrap & Co., Ltd., 1948; Hispanic Institute, Columbia University, "El Señor don Gato," "La Torre de Alicante," and "Al Olivo Subí," from *Folk Music and Poetry of Spain and Portugal,* collected by Kurt Schindler; Edward B. Marks Music Corporation for "El Rancho Grande," Copyright Edward B. Marks Music Corporation, used by permission; Organization of American States, Washington, D.C., for "Vamos a la Mar," "El Sapo," "Hojita de Guarumal," and "Mi Pollera"; University of Mexico, for "Señora Santa Ana" and "Miren Cuántas Luces," from *Panorama de la Musica Tradicional de Mexico* by Vincente T. Mendoza.

I would also like to thank the following libraries and individuals for the help they have given me in preparing this book: The New York Public Library, Music Division, Special Collections, The Lincoln Center Library and Museum of the Performing Arts; The Greenwich (Connecticut) Library; The New York Society Library; Joyce Kelley, for her assistance in playing the songs and her advice regarding the music; David Jessie, for preparing the guitar chords; Camellia Yanes, for checking Spanish usage and English translations; and my husband, Harlow Rockwell, for his help with the mechanical preparation of the book.

A. R.

Library of Congress Cataloging-in-Publication Data El Toro pinto and other songs in Spanish / selected and illustrated by Anne Rockwell. — 1st Aladdin Paperbacks ed. p. of music Melodies with chord symbols. Includes English translations. ISBN 0-689-71880-2 1. Children's songs. 2. Folk songs, Spanish. [1. Songs. 2. Folk songs. 3. Spanish language materials.] I. Rockwell, Anne F., ill.
M1997.T78 1995 94-6954

para
Ana, Isabel y Oliviero

Contents

Contents

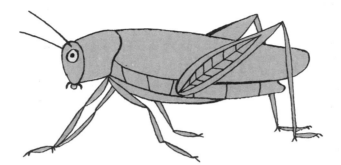

A Note About the Songs

Spanish is spoken as a first language by more people outside the country of its origin than any other language except English. The songs in this collection have been gathered from almost all the countries where Spanish is spoken—from Spain itself to Latin America and the United States. The songs "Cielito Lindo" and "El Rancho Grande" are truly folk songs from the southwestern United States, and are popular among the Spanish-American people of Texas, Arizona, and New Mexico. In the Latin American songs, while the language is Spanish, the rhythms and melodies come from many sources. The complex rhythms of Africa are there, especially in the music of Cuba, Venezuela, and Panama, giving it a rhythm we think of as characteristically Latin American. Peru has folk songs where the words are Spanish but the plaintive, mournful melodies are pure Indian and tell us much of the Pre-Columbian music of the Incas and how it must have sounded. Mexican music combines Indian and Spanish melodies, then adds the elegant patterns of the waltz and minuet, brought to Mexico from the ballrooms of Paris and Vienna during the reign of Emperor Maximilian in the nineteenth century. Argentina's songs, while basically Spanish, have been influenced by the gay, melodic music introduced by the large numbers of Italians who have been emigrating to that country for the past hundred years. But of all the Spanish-speaking countries of America, it is Puerto Rico whose music is closest to the music of Spain.

Spanish music itself represents two continents. In northern Spain the influences are European, and the music resembles that of Spain's neighbors, France and Portugal, more than it does the music of southern Spain. For southern Spain was long the home of the Moors in the Middle Ages and earlier, and the music of that region has the long-held wailing note and key shifts characteristic of North African and Arabic music. Such a song is the lovely lullaby "Niña, Nana."

An ancient Spanish Christmas carol is included that goes back at least to the twelfth century: "Baile de Nadal." As the words of this old song are very different from the language spoken in Spain today, the modern Spanish version on page 51 may be helpful to the reader. This translation is not meant to be sung.

Because the songs come from such different cultures, not all of them are equally easy to sing. However, there are many that can be easily learned and enjoyed by the very youngest of Spanish-speaking children, or by those English-speaking children who are just beginning to learn Spanish as a second language. Some of the simplest in this collection are "El Señor don Gato," "Arroz con Leche," "Al Olivo Subí," "El Zancudo," "Mi Pollera," "La Torre de Alicante," "Señora Santa Ana," "¡Jeu! ¡Jeu!" "Era una Vez," and "Hojita de Guarumal."

Guitar chords have been added as accompaniment for most of the songs. However, many of them are appropriate for various rhythm accompaniments, such as tambourines, castanets, gourd rattles, bongo drums, and steel drums. Two songs that would be very effective with a rhythm band and accompaniment are "Vamos a la Mar" and "La Burriquita." Still another instrument that could accompany the voice in many songs is the xylophone, used as a substitute for the traditional South American marimba.

The costumes and architecture, plants and animals represented in the illustrations have been carefully researched, and are like those to be found in the countries from which the songs come. When a song can be placed in time, the costumes represent the style of dress of the period. For example, "Má Teodora" sings of a historic person—a freed black woman who was a well-known dancer in seventeenth century Cuba—and her costume in the illustration represents that era. Many of the songs could be used within plays or puppet shows planned and performed by children; a number of adventures of the well-dressed cat, "El Señor don Gato," could be improvised by children, and in fact are throughout Spain, for he is a well-known figure of Spanish folklore. "Miren Cuántas Luces" could be a beautiful Christmas tableau with the Mexican shepherds and their flower-decked sombreros. It is hoped that the costumes in the book can serve as reference material for children who wish to make costumes or puppets.

For those children who are just learning Spanish, the pictures are there to suggest what the song is about and to give them hints as to the meaning of the Spanish words. (English translations, not intended for singing, are provided on pages 41 through 52.) For Spanish-speaking children, the pictures are there for fun, just as singing the songs is fun, and to reflect the mood and flavor of a song and the culture from which it comes. As for the songs themselves, some are sad, some are happy, some are funny, and some are all these things at once.

¡Ahora vamos a cantar!

ANNE ROCKWELL

El Toro Pinto

É—cha-me e-se to-ro pin-to, hi—jo de la va-ca mo-ra. Para sa-car-le u-na suer-te, de—lan-te de mi se—ño—ra.
¡Qué te co-ge el to—ro, Si-mo-na! ¡Qué te co-ge el to—ro, Mar-ce-la!

Mi Pollera

Mi po—lle—ra, mi po——lle—ra, mi po——lle—ra es co—lo—ra—da. Yo quie—ro u—na po——lle—ra de holán de co—co. Si tú no me las das, me voy con o—tro. 2. Mi po— ti—go

Verses 1 & 2   Verse 3

2. Mi pollera, mi pollera,
    Mi pollera es colorada.
    La tuya es blanca, la mía es rosada,
    Mi pollera es colorada.

3. Mi pollera, mi pollera,
    Mi pollera es colorada.
    Yo quiero una pollera de holán de hilo.
    Si tú me la das, me voy contigo.

El Señor don Gato

Es – ta–ba el se–ñor don Ga–to, o–le plum, sen–ta–di–to en su te – ja–do.

O – le plum, ca–ta–plúm, ca–ta — plúm. Es–ta–ba el señor don Ga–to, o – le

plum, sen–ta–di–to en su te — ja–do. O–le plum, ca–ta–plúm, ca–ta–plúm.

3

El Carite

A-yer sa—lió la lancha *Nueva Esparta.* Sa-lió con-fia-da a

re-co-rrer los ma-res. Encontró un pez de fuerzas muy li—ge-ro que a-

ga-rra los an-zue-los y re-vien-ta los gua-ra—les. Encontró un pez de

fuerzas muy li—ge-ro que a-ga-rra los an-zue-los y re-vien-ta los gua-ra-les.

¡Có — mo la costa es bo-ni-ta! Yo me ven — go di-vir—tien-do pe-ro

me vie—ne si—guien-do de fue—ra u-na pi-ra—gui-ta.

2. Ayer salimos muy temprano a pescar.
Nos fuimos juntos todos los pescadores.
Y entra las olas lo vimos saltando
Que iba persiguiendo a los voladores.
Y entra las olas lo vimos saltando
Que iba persiguiendo a los voladores.
¡Cómo la costa es bonita! *Etc*. . . .

3. Un marinero al verlo se alegró
A este sabroso pescado de los mares,
Y en seguida les dijo a los muchachos,
«¡Preparen los arpones y tiren los guarales!»
Y en seguida les dijo a los muchachos,
«¡Preparen los arpones y tiren los guarales!»
¡Cómo la costa es bonita! *Etc*. . . .

4. En los ramales del coco lo pescamos
En lo profundo del mar donde vivía.
Y lo pescamos en la lancha *Nueva Esparta*
Para presentarlo hoy con alegría.
Y lo pescamos en la lancha *Nueva Esparta*
Para presentarlo hoy con alegría.
¡Cómo la costa es bonita! *Etc*. . . .

5. Señores todos les damos las gracias
Los pescadores se van a marchar.
Nos despedimos con este Carite
Que les presentamos en este lugar.
Nos despedimos con este Carite
Que les presentamos en este lugar.
¡Cómo la costa es bonita! *Etc*. . . .

NUE

5

La Burriquita

Ya vie-ne la bu-rri—qui-ta, ya vie-ne do-mes-ti—cá. Ya

vie-ne la bu-rri—qui-ta, ya vie-ne do-mes-ti—cá. No le teman a la

bu-rra que no es la bu-rra ma—niá. No le te-man a la bu-rra que no es

la bu-rra ma—niá. Ay sí, ay no. Ma-ri—qui-ta me re-ga—

ló un ca——na-rio que can—ta-ba los ver—sos del Ni—ño

Dios. Un ca——na-rio que can-ta-ba los ver—sos del Ni—ño Dios.

La Torre de Alicante

En A—li—can—te ha su—ce—di — do la to-rre nue-va que se ha ca-
í — do. En A—li—can-te ha su—ce—di — do la to-rre
nue-va que se ha ca—í — do. H, I, J, K, Ll, Ñ, M, A. Que si us-
ted no me quie-re, o—tro a—man—te me que —— rrá.

2. En el lugar donde vivo
   Triste padezco, llorando.
   A este barrio he venido
   A divertirme cantando.

3. ¡Todos, toditos, arriba!
   ¡El carnaval ha llegado!
   Domingo, lunes y martes,
   Tres días y se acabó.

9

Arroz con Leche

Allegretto

(Chorus) A-rroz con le—che; me quie-ro ca—sar con u-na viu-di-ta de la ca-pi—tal, que se-pa co-ser, que se-pa bor-dar, que ponga la mesa en su san-to lu-gar. (Solo) Yo soy la viu—di-ta, la hi-ja del Rey. Me quie-ro ca—sar y no ha—llo con quien. Con-ti—go, sí. Con-ti-go, no. (Chorus) Con-ti-go, mi vi-da, me ca-sa-ré vo.

Hay Aquí, Madre, un Jardín

Hay a — quí, ma-dre, un jar — dín no muy le — jos de mi es —
tan-cia. Hay a — quí, madre, un jar — dín no muy le — jos de mi es —
tan-cia. Pim pi — rim pim pi — rim pim pim pim. Donde es-par-cen su fra —
gran — cia la dia — me — la y el jaz — mín. Es ver — dad.

2. El zunzún y el tomeguín
   Liban la blanca azucena,
   Que en bella tarde serena
   Mágico perfume exhala.
   Pim pirim pim pirim pim pim pim.
   Y crecen con toda gala
   El clavel y la verbena.
   Es verdad.

A Cantar a una Niña

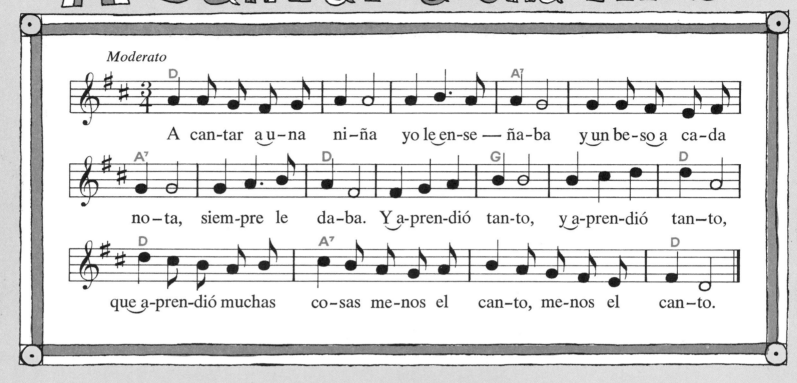

Moderato

A can-tar a u-na ni-ña yo le en-se — ña-ba y un be-so a ca-da no-ta, siem-pre le da-ba. Y a-pren-dió tan-to, y a-pren-dió tan-to, que a-pren-dió muchas co-sas me-nos el can-to, me-nos el can-to.

Ho — ji — ta de gua-ru — mal, don-de vi—ve la lan — gos-ta, don-de
co-me, don-de duer-me, don-de vi—ve la lan — gos-ta.

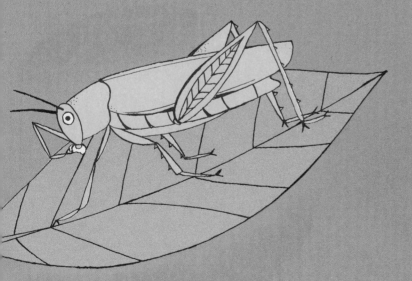

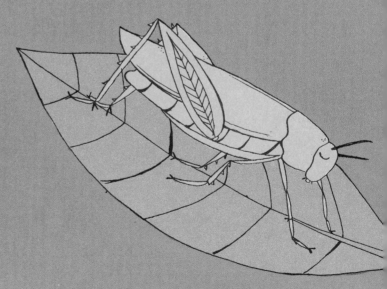

13

El Sol y la Luna

Allegro moderato

El sol se lla—ma Lo—ren—zo, ti—bi—tón, y la lu—na

Ca—ta——li—na. An—dan siem—pre se—pa—ra—dos

por dis—gus—tos de fa——mi—lia. Con el ti—bi, ti—bi, ti—bi,

ti—bi, ti—bi—tón. Con el ti—bi, ti—bi, ti—bi, ti—bi, se a—ca—bó.

2. El sol le dijo a la luna: «Tibitón,
   No presumas demasiado,
   Que el vestido en que luces
   De limosna te lo han dado.»
   Con el tibi, *etc.* . . .

3. El sol le dijo a la luna: «Tibitón,
   No quiero nada contigo;
   Pasas la noche en la calle
   Con ladrones y bandidos.»
   Con el tibi, *etc.* . . .

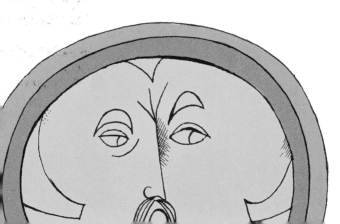

Señora Santa Ana

Se-ño-ra San-ta A-na, ¿por qué llo-ra el ni-ño? Por u-na man-
za-na que se le ha per—di-do. Se-ño-ra San-ta A-na ¿por qué llo-ra el
ni-ño? Por u-na man-za-na que se le ha per—di-do. Duér-ma-se,
ni-ño, duér-ma-se ya, que ahí vie-ne el vie-jo y se lo lle-va——rá.

2. Vamos a la huerta, cortaremos dos.
Una para el niño, y otra para vos.
Vamos a la huerta, cortaremos dos.
Una para el niño, y otra para vos.
Duérmase niño, duérmase ya,
Que ahí viene el viejo y se lo lleverá.

Dime, Lluvia

¿Di-me, llu-via, si ya se di — vi-san los ce-rros, los ce-rros de mi pue-blo; a—que-llos ce-rros que de—bo ca—mi-nar, y las flo—res que de—bo re — co — ger?

La Panaderita

Vivace con brio

A la en-tra-da del pue-blo y a la sa-li—da, hay u—
na pa-na—de-ra, pa—na-de-ri—ta, pa-na-de-ri—ta. ¡Qué pa-na—
de-ra lin—da y chi-qui-ta, qué pa-na—de-ra, pa—na—de—ri—ta!

2. Al besarla le ha dicho hoy, su abuelita:
   Eres sabrosa, niña, como la miga, como la miga.
   ¡Qué panadera, linda y chiquita,
   Qué panadera, panaderita!

Má Teodora

(Solo) «¿Dónde es-tá la Má Teo-do-ra?» (Chorus) «Ra —— jan-do la le-ña es-

tá.» (Solo) «¿Con su pa-lo y su ban-dola?» (Chorus) «Ra-jan-do la le-ña es-

tá.» (Solo) «¿Dónde está que no la veo?» (Chorus) «Ra-jan-do la le-ña es-

tá, ra —— jan-do la le-ña es — tá, ra — jan-do la le-ña es — tá.»

El Sapo

El sa-po es un a — ni — mal, que no tie-ne buen ta–lan-te. Chimi-chimi–ni-que, chimi-chimi — ni-que. ¡Que no tie-ne buen ta-lan-te, eh! Pe-ro en su con-ver — sa — ción pue-de ser un co-man-dan-te. Chimi-chimi–ni-que, chimi-chimi — ni-que. ¡Pue-de ser un co-man-dan-te, eh!

2. Cuando está en sociedad,
   Siempre su presensia grata.
   Chimi-chiminique, chimi-chiminique.
   ¡Siempre su presencia grata, eh!
   Haciendo genuflexiones
   Y hablando pura lata.
   Chimi-chiminique, chimi-chiminique.
   ¡Y hablando pura lata, eh!

3. En el amor es experto,
   Y en eso tiene el secreto.
   Chimi-chiminique, chimi-chiminique.
   ¡Y en eso tiene el secreto, oh!
   Enemigo del trabajo,
   Muy bailador y discreto.
   Chimi-chiminique, chimi-chiminique.
   ¡Muy bailador y discreto, oh!

21

Al Canto de una Laguna

Al can — to de u-na la — gu-na   he cri-a-do u-na tro-pa'e vi — cu-ñas.

Al can — to de u-na la-gu-na   he cri-a-do u — na tro-pa'e vi — cu-ñas.

Al mo-men-to de mi re-ti-ra-da   no hay quien me a-com-pa-ñe a llo-rar.

Al mo-men-to de mi re-ti-ra-da   no hay quien me a-com-pa-ñe a llo-rar.

El Rancho Grande

A—llá en el ran-cho gran-de, a—llá don-de vi—ví—a, ha—

bía u-na ran-che—ri—ta, que a-le-gre me de—cí—a, que a-le-gre me de—

Verse

cí—a: «Voy a ha-cer-te u-nos cal—zo-nes, co-mo los que u-sa el ran-che-ro.

Te los co-mien-zo de la-na y los a-ca-bo de cue-ro.»

El Tortillero

2. Bella ingrata, no respondes
   A mi grito placentero
   Cuando pasa por tu casa,
   Pregonando el tortillero.
   Mas voy cantando, con harta pena:
   Quien compra mis tostaítas,
   Tortillas buenas.

3. Ya me voy a retirar
   Con mi canasto y farol,
   Sin tener tu compasión
   De este pobre tortillero.
   Mas voy contando, con harta pena:
   Quien compra mis tostaítas,
   Tortillas buenas.

25

Al Olivo Subí

Allegretto semplice

Al o—li-vo, al o—li-vo, y al o—li-vo su—bí. Por cor—
tar u—na ra—ma del o—li-vo ca—í. Del o—li-vo ca—
í. ¿Quién me le—van-ta—rá? Y e-sa ga-chí mo-re—na que la
ma—no me da, que la ma-no me da. Que la ma-no me
dio, y e-sa ga-chi mo—re—na es la que quie-ro yo.

Cielito Lindo

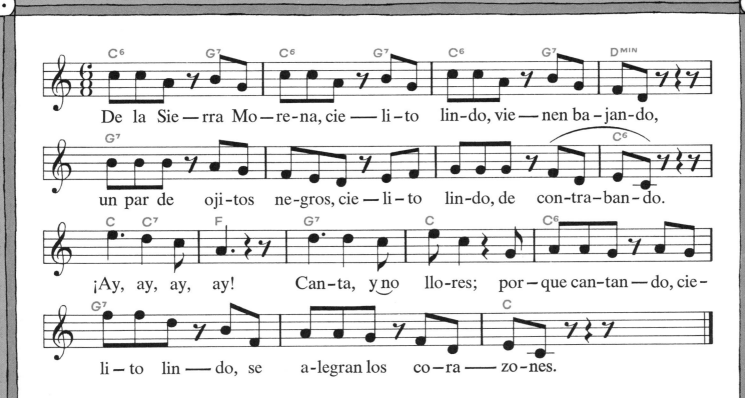

De la Sie — rra Mo — re-na, cie — li-to   lin-do, vie — nen ba-jan-do,

un par de   oji-tos   ne-gros, cie — li-to   lin-do, de   con-tra-ban-do.

¡Ay, ay, ay,   ay!   Can-ta, y no   llo-res;   por — que can-tan — do, cie-

li — to   lin — do, se   a-legran los   co-ra — zo-nes.

2. Un flecha en el aire, cielito lindo, lanzó cupido,
   Y esa flecha volando, cielito lindo, bien me ha herido.
   ¡Ay, ay, ay, ay! Canta, y no llores;
   Porque cantando, cielito lindo,
   Se alegran los corazones.

El Zancudo

E —ché mis pe-rros al mon-te. El u—no la-dró muy

du—ro. El a—mo se fue a a-so-mar y er' un in-fe—liz zan—

cu—do. 2. Cla—vé mi ro—di—lla en tie—rra y a-pun-té bi-en a—

pun-tao, y fue tan grand'el ba —la-zo que que-dó pa-ta-rri—bia—o.

3. El zancudo cayó al mar
   Y se quedó en un remanso.
   Mil metros tenía de hondo
   Y una pata dabo al Cabo.

4. Pa matar ese animal
   Se tendió l'infantería
   Con quince ametralladoras
   Y un cañón d'infantería.

5. La carne d'este animal
   La mandaron pa Marmato.
   Pesaba dos mil arrobas,
   Catorce libras y cuarto.

6. El sebo d'este animal
   Lo mandaron p'al Tabor.
   Eso hace quinientos años,
   Y todavía hay jabón.

7. Del cuero d'ese animal
   Salieron dos mil paraguas,
   Y un pedazo que sobró
   Se lu'hizo una vieja en naguas.

29

Vamos a la Mar

Va-mos a la mar, tum tum, a co-mer pes — ca-do, tum tum;

bo-ca co — lo — ra-da, tum tum, fri — ti-to y a — sa-do, tum tum.

2. Vamos a la mar, tum tum,
    A comer pescado, tum tum,
    Fritito y asado, tum tum,
    En sartén de palo, tum tum.

Niña, Nana

A la na-ni-ta, na-ni-ta, a la na-ni-ta de a-
quel que lle-vó el ca-ba-llo al a-gua, y lo
tra-jo sin be-ber.

2. Duérmete, niño chiquito,
Duérmete y no llores más,
Que reirán los angelitos
Para no verte llorar.

Mi Compadre Mono

Mi com-pa-dre mo-no tie-ne dos ca—mi-sas; u—na que li'a-planchan yo-tra que li'a—li-san. ¡Va-lien-te mo-no, tan des-ca—ra—do que no res——pe—ta! Por ir a be—sar la no-via be-só a la sue-gra yal-zó la ma-no y le dio en la je—ta.

2. Mi compadre mono
Tiene dos calzones;
Unos de bayeta
Y otros sin botones.
¡Valiente mono,
Tan descarado
Que no respeta!
Por ir a besar la novia
Besó a la suegra
Y alzó la mano
Y le dio en la jeta.

3. Allá van los monos
Por la travesía
A alcanzar el baile
De Juana María.
¡Valiente mono,
Tan descarado
Que no respeta!
Por ir a besar la novia
Besó a la suegra
Y alzó la mano
Y le dio en la jeta.

33

Era una Vez

Allegretto

E—ra u—na vez un bar-co chi-qui—ti-to, e—ra u—na
vez un bar-co chi-qui—ti-to, e—ra u—na vez un bar-co chi-qui—
ti—to, que no po—dí—a, que no po—dí—a, que no po—
dí—a ca—mi—nar. Pa-sa-ron u—na, dos, tres, cuatro, cinco, seis, sie-te se—
ma-nas, pa-sa-ron u—na, dos, tres, cuatro, cinco, seis, sie-te se—ma-nas,
pa-sa-ron u—na, dos, tres, cuatro, cinco, seis, sie-te se—ma-nas, y los
ví—ve-res, y los ví—ve-res em-pe——za-ron a es-ca——sear.

Se pusieron,
Se pusieron,
Se pusieron a pescar

2. Los tripulantes de este barquito,
   Los tripulantes de este barquito,
   Los tripulantes de este barquito

Pescaron peces grandes, chicos, y medianos,
Pescaron peces grandes, chicos, y medianos,
Pescaron peces grandes, chicos, y medianos,

Y se pusieron,
Y se pusieron,
Y se pusieron a cenar.

35

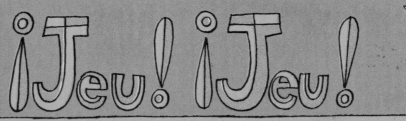

¡Jeu! ¡Jeu!

Allegro giocoso

Por a — quí pa-só u-na pa-va, chi-qui — ti-ta y vo-la-

do — ra. Qu'en las a — las lle-va flo — res,

y'en el pi — co mis a —— mo — res. ¡Jeu! ¡Jeu!

Baile de Nadal

Allegro

A vin-ti-cinc de De-sem-bre, fum, fum, fum, a vin-ti-cinc de De-sem-bre,

fum, fum, fum, ha nas — cut un mi-nyo-net ros i blan — quet, ros i blan-

quet. Fill de la Ver – ge Ma — ri – a, n'és nat en u-na e-sta — bli – a, fum, fum,

fum! Ha nas — cut un mi-nyo — net ros i blan-quet, ros i blan-quet. Fill de

la Ver – ge Ma — ri – a, n'és nat en u-na e-sta — bli – a, fum, fum, fum!

Miren Cuántas Luces

Mi-ren cuán-tas lu—ces, cuán—tos res-plan—do-res. Sin du-da es Be-

lén. ¡Qué glo-ria, pas—to-res! ¡Qué glo—ria, pas—to-res!

2. Ándale, Batito,
   Chíflale al ganado.
   Vamos a dar agua
   Al Río Colorado.
   Al Río Colorado.

3. ¡Qué cerros tan altos!
   Lindos nos parece;
   Junten el ganado
   Porque ya amanece.
   Porque ya amanece.

4. Camina, Gilita,
   Que vendrás cansada;
   Por aquellos montes
   Haremos posada.
   Haremos posada.

5. Qué bonitas flores
   Hay por este cerro.
   Córtalas, Gilita,
   Para tu sombrero.
   Para tu sombrero.

6. ¡Albricias, pastores!
   Ya el gallo cantó.
   Clarito nos dice:
   «¡Ya Cristo nació!
   ¡Ya Cristo nació!»

7. Areen la mulita,
   Bájenle el huacal,
   Saquen los tamales
   Para calentar.
   Para calentar.

39

Translations of the Songs

El Toro Pinto (FROM PAGE 1)

The Spotted Bull

Let loose that spotted bull, son of the dark red cow,
So that I can take a chance with the cape
And show off to my lady.
The bull will toss you, Simon!
The bull will toss you, Marcel!

Mi Pollera (FROM PAGE 2)

My Hoopskirt

1. My hoopskirt, my hoopskirt,
   My hoopskirt is bright red.
   I want a hoopskirt of light brown linen.
   If you don't give me one, I'll go with another.

2. My hoopskirt, my hoopskirt,
   My hoopskirt is bright red.
   Yours is white, mine is rosy red.
   My hoopskirt is bright red.

3. My hoopskirt, my hoopskirt,
   My hoopskirt is bright red.
   I want a hoopskirt of ruffled linen.
   If you give me one, I'll go with you.

El Señor don Gato (FROM PAGE 3)

Sir Tomcat

There was Sir Tomcat, hooray!
Sitting on his roof,
Hooray!
There was Sir Tomcat, hooray!
Sitting on his roof,
Hooray!

El Carite (FROM PAGE 4)

The Carite Fish

1. The launch *New Sparta* sailed.
   It sailed confidently over the sea,
   And met a very clever fish
   Who grasped the fishhooks and broke the lines.
   And met a very clever fish
   Who grasped the fishhooks and broke the lines.
   How beautiful the coast is!
   I would like to take it easy
   But I am being followed close
   By a small boat.

2. Yesterday we sailed very early to fish.
   All of the fishermen left together.
   And between the waves we saw him leaping,
   Following the flying fish.
   And between the waves we saw him leaping,
   Following the flying fish.
   How beautiful the coast is! *Etc.* . . .

3. A sailor called out with joy
   At the sight of this tasty fish of the sea,
   And called out to all the boys,
   "Prepare the harpoons and cast the lines!"
   And called out to all the boys,
   "Prepare the harpoons and cast the lines!"
   How beautiful the coast is! *Etc.* . . .

4. In the ropes of coconut fiber we caught him,
   In the deep sea where he lived,
   And the fishermen of the *New Sparta*
   Present him today with joy.
   And the fishermen of the *New Sparta*
   Present him today with joy.
   How beautiful the coast is! *Etc.* . . .

5. Gracious gentlemen and ladies,
   Now the fishermen will leave you.
   We leave you this great Carite,
   Which we present to you here in this village.
   We leave you this great Carite,
   Which we present to you here in this village.
   How beautiful the coast is! *Etc.* . . .

La Burriquita (FROM PAGE 6)

The Little Donkey

Here comes the little donkey,
Who comes gentle and tame.
Here comes the little donkey,
Who comes gentle and tame.
Don't be afraid of the donkey;
He is not a scary donkey.
Don't be afraid of the donkey;
He is not a scary donkey.
Oh yes. Oh no.
Ladybug gave me for a gift
A canary who sings
Songs of the Child of God.
A canary who sings
Songs of the Child of God.

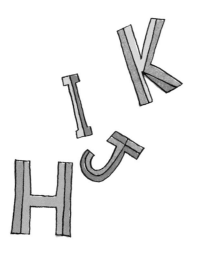

La Torre de Alicante (FROM PAGE 7)

The Tower of Alicante

In Alicante it came to pass
That the new tower tumbled down.
In Alicante it came to pass
That the new tower tumbled down.
H, I, J, K,Ll, Ñ, M, A.
If you don't want me,
Another sweetheart will.

Ahora Voy a Cantarles (FROM PAGE 8)

Now I'm Going to Sing

1. Now I'm going to sing
   Until the daylight comes.
   The merrymakers are coming here
   Down from the top of the hills.

2. In the place where I live
   I suffer from sadness and weeping.
   So I came to this town,
   To pass my time in singing.

3. Get up, everyone!
   The carnival has begun!
   Sunday, Monday, and Tuesday,
   Three days, and then it's finished.

Arroz con Leche (FROM PAGE 10)

Rice with Milk

(Chorus) Rice with milk; I want to marry
A sweet little widow from the capital city,
Who is able to sew, who is able to embroider,
And set a fine table.

(Solo) I am the pretty little widow,
And the daughter of the king.
I wish to marry, but I don't know with whom.
With you, yes. With you, no.

(Chorus) With you my love, I will marry you.

Hay Aquí, Madre, un Jardín (FROM PAGE 11)

Mother, There Is a Garden

1. Mother, there is a garden
   Not very far from my farmhouse.
   Mother, there is a garden
   Not very far from my farmhouse.
   Peem pee-reem peem pee-reem peem peem peem.
   There the fragrance fills the air
   Of the diamela and the jasmine.
   It's true.

2. The hummingbirds
   Sip at the white lily
   That in the quiet evening
   Gives off magical perfume.
   Peem pee-reem *etc. . . .*
   And growing there with festive colors
   Are the carnation and the verbena.
   It's true.

A Cantar a una Niña (FROM PAGE 12)

To Teach a Young Girl to Sing

I was teaching a young girl to sing,
And I always gave her a kiss at each note.
And she learned so much,
And she learned so much,
And she learned many things but not to sing,
But not to sing.

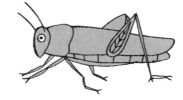

Hojita de Guarumal (FROM PAGE 13)

Little Leaf of the Guarumal

Little leaf of the guarumal,
There lives the locust,
There he eats, there he sleeps,
There lives the locust.

El Sol y la Luna (FROM PAGE 14)

The Sun and the Moon

1. The sun calls himself Lorenzo, tee-bee-ton,
   And the moon Catalina.
   They are always apart
   For their families have quarreled.
   With a tee-bee, tee-bee, tee-bee, tee-bee, tee-bee-ton.
   With a tee-bee, tee-bee, tee-bee, tee-bee, it is done.

2. The sun said to the moon: "Tee-bee-ton,
   Don't put on airs and show off
   In that shining dress
   That out of charity I gave you."
   With a tee-bee, *etc. . . .*

3. The sun said to the moon: "Tee-bee-ton,
   I would never want to go with you,
   You spend your nights in dark alleys
   With thieves and bandits."
   With a tee-bee, *etc. . . .*

Señora Santa Ana (FROM PAGE 16)

Lady Saint Anne

1. Lady Saint Anne, why does the little boy cry?
   It is for an apple that he has lost.
   Lady Saint Anne, why does the little boy cry?
   It is for an apple that he has lost.
   Sleep, little boy, sleep.
   For here comes an old man to carry you off.

2. Let us go to the orchard and we will cut two.
   One for the little boy, and the other for you.
   Let us go to the orchard and we will cut two.
   One for the little boy, and the other for you.
   Sleep, little boy, sleep.
   For here comes an old man to carry you off.

Dime, Lluvia (FROM PAGE 17)

Tell Me, Rain

Tell me, rain, can you make out the peaks,
The peaks of the mountains around my town;
Those peaks that I must cross over,
And the flowers that I must gather?

La Panaderita (FROM PAGE 18)

The Baker-Girl

1. At the entrance of the city,
   And at the exit,
   There is a baker-girl, a darling baker-girl, a darling.
   What a pretty little baker-girl,
   What a baker-girl, what a darling baker-girl!

2. Her grandmother told her today when she kissed her:
   "You are as tasty, little girl, as breadcrumbs,
   As breadcrumbs."
   What a pretty little baker-girl,
   What a baker-girl, what a darling baker-girl!

Má Teodora (FROM PAGE 19)

Má Teodora

"Where is Má Teodora?"
"Chopping firewood over there."
"With her stick and her mandolin?"
"Chopping firewood over there."
"Where is she if I don't see her?"
"Chopping firewood over there, chopping firewood over there,
chopping firewood over there, chopping firewood over there."

El Sapo (FROM PAGE 20)

The Toad

1. The toad is an animal
   Who isn't very talented.
   Cheemee-cheemeeneek, cheemee-cheemeeneek.
   Who isn't very talented!
   But in his conversation
   You'd think he was an officer.
   Cheemee *etc.* . . .
   You'd think he was an officer, hey!

2. When he's out in high society,
   He always puts on airs.
   Cheemee *etc.* . . .
   He always puts on airs, hey!
   Making bows,
   And talking nonsense.
   Cheemee *etc.* . . .
   And talking nonsense, hey!

3. In love he is an expert,
   He knows all the secrets.
   Cheemee *etc.* . . .
   He knows all the secrets, oh!
   He hates work,
   But prefers a lot of fancy dancing.
   Cheemee *etc.* . . .
   But prefers a lot of fancy dancing, oh!

Al Canto de una Laguna (FROM PAGE 22)

At the Edge of a Lagoon

At the edge of a lagoon
I raised a herd of vicunas. (repeat)
At the moment that I left there,
I had no one to accompany me in crying. (repeat)

El Rancho Grande (FROM PAGE 23)

The Big Ranch

There was a big ranch,
Where I used to live.
There was a little cow girl
Who said to me, who said to me:
"See, I've made you some chaps,
like a real rancher wears.
They start out as wool,
And end up as leather."

El Tortillero (FROM PAGE 24)

The Tortilla-Seller

1. Dark night, I see nothing.
   But I carry my lantern,
   By your doors I am passing
   And singing with love.
   But I am singing full of sorrow.
   Who will buy my baked goods?
   Good, tasty tortillas!

2. Ungrateful beauty, you don't answer
   To my joyful cry,
   When by your house passes
   This tortilla-seller crying.
   But I am singing *etc.* . . .

3. Now I am going to go away
   With my basket and my lantern,
   Without gaining your pity
   For this poor tortilla-seller.
   But I am singing *etc.* . . .

Al Olivo Subí (FROM PAGE 26)

I Climbed the Olive Tree

To the olive tree, to the olive tree,
To the top of the olive tree I climbed.
I fell down trying to cut a branch
Of the olive tree.
Who is going to help me up?
And that brown-skinned girl
Who gives me her hand, who gives me her hand,
Whose hand she gave me,
And that brown-skinned girl is the one I love.

Cielito Lindo <small>(FROM PAGE 27)</small>

Pretty Skies Above

1. From the Dark Mountain Ridges, pretty skies above,
   A pair of black eyes are descending, pretty skies above,
   Like bandits.
   Ay, ay, ay, ay!
   Sing and don't cry, pretty skies above,
   Because when you sing, pretty skies above,
   It makes hearts gay.

2. A flash in the air, pretty skies above,
   Cupid's arrow with a flying flash, pretty skies above,
   Has wounded me.
   Ay, ay, ay, ay! *Etc.* . . .

El Zancudo <small>(FROM PAGE 28)</small>

The Mosquito

1. I set my dogs loose on the hill.
   One of them barked very loud.
   The boss looked to see what it was,
   There was an unhappy mosquito.

2. I dug my knee into the ground,
   And aimed straight and true.
   And the bullet hit so hard,
   That it knocked him off his feet.

3. The mosquito fell in the sea,
   And got stuck in the still water.
   A thousand meters deep he was,
   And one of his feet was ashore at Cabo.

4. To kill this animal,
   They used the whole infantry,
   With fifteen machine guns,
   And an infantry cannon.

5. The flesh of this animal
   They ordered it sent to Marmato.
   It weighed two thousand arrobas,*
   Forty pounds, and a quarter.

6. The fat of this animal,
   They ordered it sent to Tabor.
   That was five hundred years ago,
   And today they still have soap.

7. The skin of this animal
   Made two thousand umbrellas.
   And a piece that was left
   Kept an old woman in petticoats.

* [a Spanish weight of twenty-five pounds]

Vamos a la Mar (FROM PAGE 30)

Let's Go to the Sea

1. Let's go to the sea, tum tum,
   To eat fish, tum tum,
   Bright-colored mouths, tum tum,
   Fried and roasted, tum tum.

2. Let's go to the sea, tum tum,
   To eat fish, tum tum,
   Fried and roasted, tum tum,
   In a wooden frying pan, tum tum.

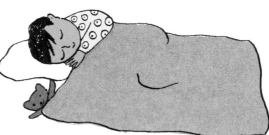

Niña, Nana (FROM PAGE 31)

Lullaby

1. This is a lullaby, lullaby,
   A lullaby of someone who
   Took his horse to water,
   And could not get him to drink.

2. Sleep, little boy,
   Sleep and cry no more.
   It makes the little angels laugh
   When they do not see you cry.

Mi Compadre Mono <small>(FROM PAGE 32)</small>

My Godfather Monkey

1. My godfather Monkey
   Has two shirts.
   One is ironed,
   The other is smooth.
   Valiant Monkey,
   So impudent
   He respects no one!
   On his way to kiss his bride
   He kissed his mother-in-law,
   Gave her a slap
   And made a face.

2. My godfather Monkey
   Has two pairs of trousers;
   One of flannel,
   And the other without buttons.
   Valiant Monkey *etc.* . . . .

3. There go the monkeys
   Toward the road
   To follow the dance
   Of Juana Maria.
   Valiant Monkey *etc.* . . . .

Era una Vez <small>(FROM PAGE 34)</small>

There Was Once

1. There was once a tiny little boat,
   There was once a tiny little boat,
   There was once a tiny little boat,
   That could not, could not, could not move.
   One, two, three, four, five, six, seven weeks passed,
   One, two, three, four, five, six, seven weeks passed,
   One, two, three, four, five, six, seven weeks passed,
   And the supplies, and the supplies began to give out.

2. The sailors of this little boat,
   The sailors of this little boat,
   The sailors of this little boat,
   Set themselves to,
   Set themselves to,
   Set themselves to fishing.
   They caught fishes, big, little, and middle-sized.
   They caught fishes, big, little, and middle-sized.
   They caught fishes, big, little, and middle-sized.
   And they set themselves to, and they set themselves to eating.

¡Jeu! ¡Jeu! <small>(FROM PAGE 36)</small>

Hay-Hoo! Hay-Hoo!

For here comes a turkey,
Very tiny, flying by.
Her wings are carrying flowers,
And she pecks a song of my loves.
Hay-Hoo! Hay-Hoo!

Baile de Nadal <small>(FROM PAGE 37)</small>

Christmas Dance

On the twenty-fifth of December, fum, fum, fum,
On the twenty-fifth of December, fum, fum, fum,
Was born a tiny one, rosy and white, rosy and white.
The Son of the Virgin Mary, He was born in a stable,
Fum, fum, fum!
Was born a tiny one, rosy and white, rosy and white.
The Son of the Virgin Mary, He was born in a stable,
Fum, fum, fum!

The modern Spanish translation reads:

"Baile de Navidad" El vienticinco de deciembre, fum, fum, fum,
a vienticinco de deciembre, fum, fum, fum, ha nacido un
niñito rosado y blanco, rosado y blanco. Hijo de la Virgen
María, fué nacido en un establo, fum, fum, fum! Ha nacido un
niñito rosado y blanco, rosado y blanco. Hijo de la Virgen
María, fué nacido en un establo, fum, fum, fum!

Miren Cuántas Luces (FROM PAGE 38)

Behold How Many Lights

1. Behold how many lights
   Are sparkling so bright.
   Without doubt it is Bethlehem.
   What glory, shepherds!
   What glory, shepherds!

2. Go on, Batito,
   Gather the herd.
   We will give them water
   At the Colorado River.
   At the Colorado River.

3. How high these peaks are!
   Beautiful they appear.
   Assemble the herd now,
   For dawn is coming.
   For dawn is coming.

4. Travel on, Gilita,
   Although you are tired,
   For in these mountains
   We are going to stop.
   We are going to stop.

5. What beautiful flowers
   Grow on this mountain.
   Pick some, Gilita,
   For your sombrero.
   For your sombrero.

6. Dawn has come, shepherds,
   And the rooster sings.
   Clearly he tells us:
   "Now Christ is born!
   Now Christ is born!"

7. Stop the donkey,
   Put down the boxes.
   Take out the tamales
   To warm them up.
   To warm them up.

The art was prepared in black and white line drawings with color overlays for benday tints. The music was lettered by Harlow Rockwell. The typeface is Times Roman, with the song titles hand lettered. The book is printed in black, yellow, red, blue and brown.